MAYBE A MONSTER

Story • Jill Creighton
Pictures • Ruth Ohi

Annick Press Ltd.
Toronto, Canada M2M 1H9

Design and graphic
realization Ruth Ohi

Annick Press gratefully acknowledges
the support of The Canada Council
and the Ontario Arts Council

Canadian Cataloguing in Publication Data

Creighton, Jill
    Maybe a monster

ISBN 1-55037-037-5 (bound) ISBN 1-55037-036-7 (pbk.)

I. Ohi, Ruth. II. Title.

PS8555.R443M39   1989   jC813'.54   C88-095351-9
PZ7.C74Ma   1989

Distributed in Canada and the USA by:

Firefly Books Ltd.
250 Sparks Ave.
Willowdale, Ontario
M2H 2S4

Printed and bound in Canada
by D.W. Friesen & Sons

For Tom and Anna

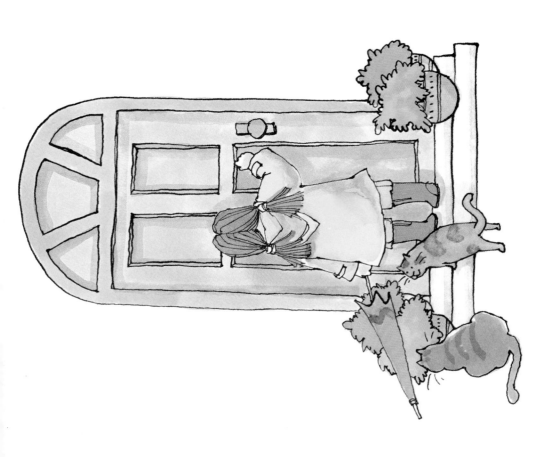

On rainy days Mary plays at Sam's house.
Today they take out all the building supplies: bricks, blocks, towers, logs, roofs, arches, a ramp, and a clock.
"Let's build a town," says Sam.

"Okay," says Mary. "We need the transport truck to carry logs, and the dump truck. And all the people can watch."

"We need an ice cream store," says Sam. "And we need a monster wall. For protection."

"Protection from what?" asks Mary.

"Maybe dinosaurs," says Sam. "Maybe giants. Maybe a monster."

"Okay," says Mary, "here's a big mountain. Let's put it right here."

They build a long monster wall from the biggest blocks, with lookout towers and soldiers on top waving flags.

"I hope it's big enough and tall enough," says Sam. "Now let's make the town."

They build a food store and a gas station, an ice cream store and a tractor store where people can buy all sorts of big machines.

Sam's church has a clock on it and Mary is building a school.

"Listen," she says. "What can I hear?"

"Giants?" asks Sam.

"It's trumpets," says Mary. "A parade is coming."

"Right into town," says Sam. "Look at the dancing chicken." There are horses prancing, and a beautiful lady twirling. There is a roly-poly clown, and an elephant carrying a great king. A policeman keeps the crowd back and soldiers with trumpets march near the end.

"The people love it," says Mary. "They're cheering and clapping."

"That guy over there is whistling and stamping his feet," says Sam.

"He always makes a lot of noise at parades," says Mary.

All of a sudden . . . WHOOSH . . . Two big furry shapes streak through, . . . right through the crowd. Everyone goes flying.

"Stop them!" cries Mary. "They're wrecking the parade."

"Tigers," yells Sam, "escaping from the zoo!"

"Let's capture them," shouts Mary.

They jump over the people, over the mountain, and chase after the ferocious tigers. But the tigers have vanished, so Mary and Sam go back to their town.

"It's lucky they weren't hungry," says Sam.

They help all the people stand up. The parade gets together and stops for a rest at the edge of town.

"Here comes the dump truck delivering more bricks," says Sam.

Mary starts work repairing her school. Sam mends the monster wall.

"Schools have flags," says Mary. She looks for an extra one.

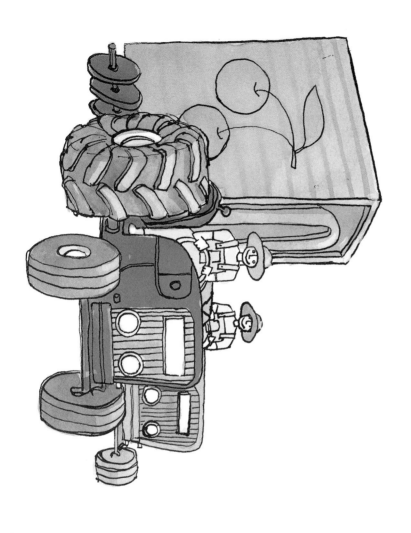

Sam fixes his church and the tractor store. He lines up the tractors outside the front door.

Suddenly they hear a gurgling, burbling, roaring sound.

"What's that?" asks Mary.

"I don't know," says Sam. "Maybe a monster."

The hills start shaking, rocks and trees come thundering down, and over the mountain comes Baby Monster.

Her hair sticks up in points and her little paws are ready. She smashes through the monster wall and slithers into town.

The people are frightened, so Sam and Mary help them hide.

Then they come back to save their town. First they yell and wave their arms and they trap Baby Monster in a monster cage. But then the Monster Control Officer arrives.

"Don't hurt that monster," she says, "she is protected by law."

So they put on their tiger suits. They growl at the monster and show her their claws. But she isn't afraid. She chews some bricks and drools. Baby Monster is hungry. Sam and Mary run to get some food.

When they come back Baby Monster throws down the bricks and grabs a cookie. She starts crunching and munching and dribbling and wiping crumbs through her hair.

"Let's haul her back up the mountain," says Sam. So they pick her up carefully and drag her over. "Push her up," says Mary, but Baby Monster growls at them and burps. Then she crawls up and vanishes with her food over the top.

Sam and Mary set out treats all along the mountain in case Baby Monster comes back.

"Look what she did," says Mary. "It's a disaster area. Our monster wall was no good."

"Let's get rid of it," says Sam.

The front-end loader comes in to pick up the mess. The transport truck and the dump truck are ready to carry bricks and blocks and logs. There is a lot of work to do. Mary and Sam begin to call the people home and build their town again.

But first they make a house just big enough for a monster.